Made in the USA
Monee, IL
20 January 2023

25773799R00057